S0-ABQ-461

Angel Friends

 TARA WILLIAMS

tate publishing
CHILDREN'S DIVISION

Published by Tate Publishing & Enterprises, LLC
127 E. Trade Center Terrace | Mustang, Oklahoma 73064 USA
1.888.361.9473 | www.tatepublishing.com

Tate Publishing is committed to excellence in the publishing industry. The company reflects the philosophy established by the founders, based on Psalm 68:11,
"The Lord gave the word and great was the company of those who published it."

Book design copyright © 2015 by Tate Publishing, LLC. All rights reserved.
Cover and interior design by Eileen Cueno
Illustrations by Lucent Ouano

Published in the United States of America
ISBN: 978-1-68097-760-8
Juvenile Fiction / Religious / Christian / Friendship
14.12.19

This Book Belongs To:

_____

"Tea for you and tea for me. *La la la la la la. We're best friends like friends should be. La la la la la la.*"

"India!" called her mother. "What is my little sweetie up to now?" as she tripped over toys, almost spilling the clean clothes from the basket she was carrying.

"Mommy, please be careful!" said five-year-old India. "Julia and I are having a tea party, and you almost spilled the tea."

"Julia? Who is Julia?" questioned her mother as she sat on the soft fairy bedspread to catch her breath.

"She's right here sitting across from me, Mommy," India giggled. "Julia would like to know if you would like to join us for tea."

"Oh, no, thank you," said Mother. "You play while I finish the laundry."

Mother opened up India's drawers and while putting clothes away listened to her daughter chat. She began to wonder about her daughter's imaginary friend. "What an imagination," she said aloud and walked out the room, shaking her head with a smile.

"Julia, Mommy doesn't believe me. Why can't Mommy see you?" asked India.

"Well," said Julia, "I am *your* special friend. Sometimes grown-ups only believe what they can see. But you believe what is in your heart, and that is very important. Come on, let's go play outside."

India and Julia whizzed by her mother in the kitchen, and India yelled, "We're going out back to play, see you soon!"

"We?" whispered India's mother, scratching her head with soap suds from washing the dishes. She then picked up another dish and continued to wash as she watched India run to her swings from the kitchen window.

"Wheeee!" yelled India. "I'm going to try and swing as high as the angels in the sky."

"Okay," said Julia, "but be very careful because angels can go very high! They fly all the way above the clouds."

"Really?" questioned India. "What else can angels do?"

Just then Julia began to sing,

"Angels fly, angels sing,
angels can do anything!

When you're sad or you're mad,
angels always make you glad!

Angels help you to believe,
ask them anytime you need,

love and laughter, lots of fun.

They will be there for anyone!

Angels are around you everyday
and every night.

Just look very close
the sparkles are so bright!

Angels fly, angels sing,
angels can do anything!"

"Wow!" said India excitedly. "Can you teach me that song?"

"Sure," said Julia, "let's go for a walk first. I have something else to show you."

As they walked through India's backyard, Julia picked up a feather off the ground.

"Here," she said, and handed India the white feather. "It's a sign from an angel. Anytime you see a feather, pick it up and all day you'll have good luck! It's an angel's way of saying hi! This feather is a special feather. It's from me to you, my best friend!"

"Thank you," smiled India. India hugged Julia and felt comforting love.

Just then it began to rain, and Julia disappeared. India looked at the beautiful feather and knew Julia would return soon.

India skipped through the rain into her house; and waving the feather, she sang, "Angels fly, angles sing, angels can do anything!"

"How was it outside, sweetie?" asked Mom.

"It was magical," said India, smiling.

"M-m-m…magical?" said Mom as she looked into her daughters eyes.

"Yes, magical! I swung high into the sky, just like an angel," said India.

"You are an angel," said her mother.

All of a sudden, Julia quietly flew by, playfully dropping a feather in the sink for India's mother to find. As she flew away, she gave India a wink. India winked back while waving her feather in the air.

"Where did this feather come from? It's like it fell from thin air," said India's mother.

"Don't be silly, Mom. It's from Julia, my best friend. She's an angel." India said.

India's mother snuggled at the table next to her daughter. "Tell me more about this angel friend, Julia? Is she here now?" Mom asked.

"Oh, no, not now, but she will be back. She visits me all the time. We play games, read books, and sing and dance together. Just listen to the song she taught me today. 'Angels fly, angels sing, angels can do anything!' Isn't it great, Mom?" India's voice was full of excitement.

"Wow," said India's mother, "sounds like you sure had lots of fun today."

"We did." Still not sure her mom believed her, India said "How about if I draw a picture of Julia for you."

"That sounds fantastic," said Mom. "Let's draw together. I'll draw for you a beautiful rainbow."

As the pitter patter of the rain stopped, a gentle breeze suddenly blew open the kitchen curtain, enough for them to see a colorful rainbow, just like the one India's mother was drawing. Above the rainbow was a beautiful sparkle of light that immediately caught India's mother's eye. She stared in wonder and amazement and felt comforting love.

"Do you see Julia, Mommy? Do you believe me now?"

India's mom felt in her heart she had an angel friend too.

listen|imagine|view|experience

AUDIO BOOK DOWNLOAD INCLUDED WITH THIS BOOK!

In your hands you hold a complete digital entertainment package. In addition to the paper version, you receive a free download of the audio version of this book. Simply use the code listed below when visiting our website. Once downloaded to your computer, you can listen to the book through your computer's speakers, burn it to an audio CD or save the file to your portable music device (such as Apple's popular iPod) and listen on the go!

How to get your free audio book digital download:

1. Visit www.tatepublishing.com and click on the e|LIVE logo on the home page.
2. Enter the following coupon code:
   d3fe-245c-816b-f7c5-eae0-d27d-2c00-5c86
3. Download the audio book from your e|LIVE digital locker and begin enjoying your new digital entertainment package today!